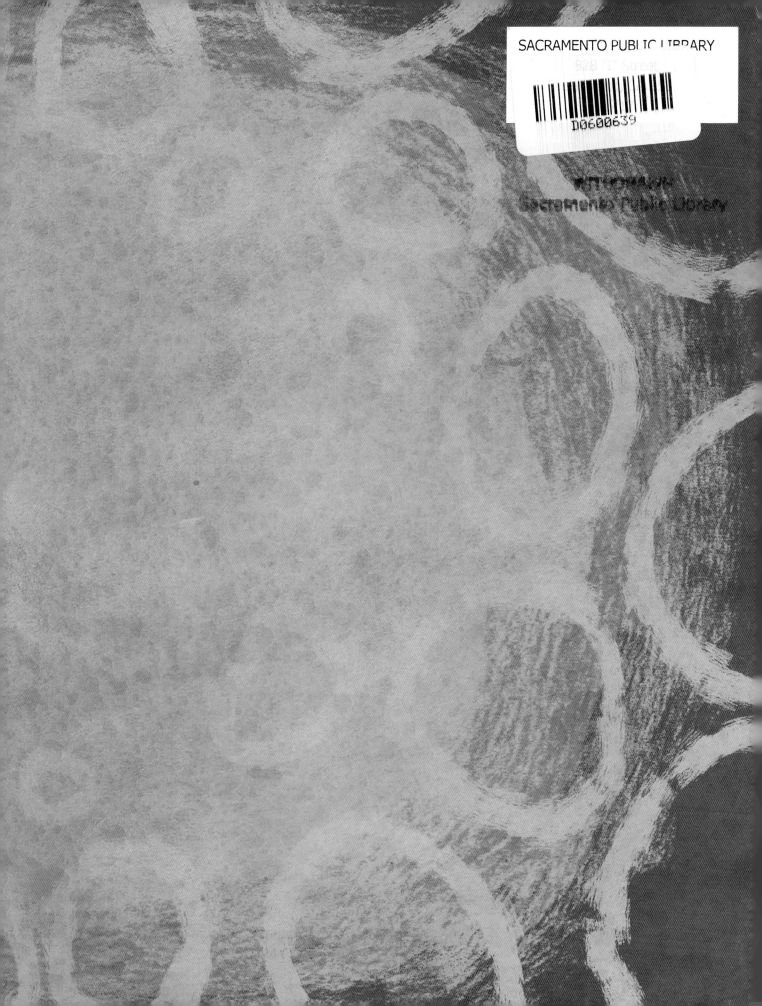

For my son and daughter.
—S.B.D.

For my wonderful Yvonne,
the Whitehouse family, and Teresa.
—B.W.

Text copyright © 2017 by Sarah Beth Durst
Illustrations copyright © 2017 by Ben Whitehouse

Printed in China

Books published by Running Press are available at special discounts for
bulk purchases in the United States by corporations, institutions, and other
organizations. For more information, please contact the Special Markets
Department at the Perseus Books Group, 2300 Chestnut Street,
Suite 200, Philadelphia, PA 19103, or call
(800) 810-4145, ext. 5000, or e-mail
special.markets@perseusbooks.com.

ISBN 978-0-7624-5986-5
Library of Congress Control Number: 2016945287

9 8 7 6 5 4 3 2 1
Digit on the right indicates the number of this printing

Designed by T.L. Bonaddio
Edited by Marlo Scrimizzi
Typography: Interstate

Published by Running Press Kids,
An imprint of Perseus Books, LLC.,
A subsidiary of Hachette Book Group, Inc.

Running Press Book Publishers
2300 Chestnut Street
Philadelphia, PA 19103–4371

Visit us on the web!
www.runningpress.com/rpkids

ROAR & SPARKLES
Go to School

by SARAH BETH DURST

Illustrated by
BEN WHITEHOUSE

RP|KIDS
PHILADELPHIA

Roar the dragon did not want summer to end.
Summer meant barbecues! Swimming with
the sea monsters! Building sand castles (and
smashing them with his tail)!

And, best of all, summer meant playing
with his big sister, Sparkles.

But fall? Fall meant the first day of school.
Roar was not sure he would like school.

"What if I have to breathe fire by myself?"
he asked Sparkles.
"Not on the first day," she told him.

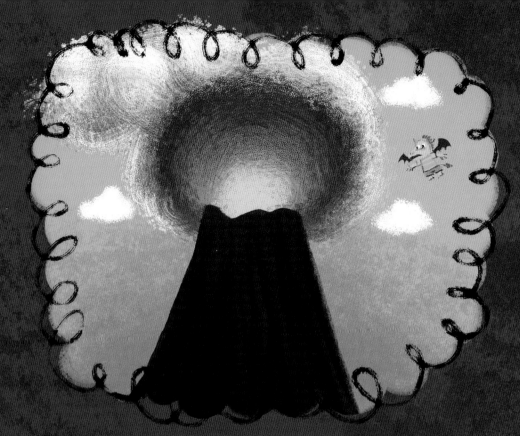

"What if I have to fly over an exploding volcano?"
"Not on the first day," she said.

"What if I have to molt my scales and grow them back
green and purple and polka-dotted?"
"Not on the first day, Roar."

"But, Sparkles, **what if** my teacher is a knight in shining armor
who doesn't like anything to do with fire,
like dragons and barbecues and even s'mores?"

Sparkles patted his scaly shoulder.
"Everyone likes s'mores. Don't worry, Roar.
It's only school. You'll like it."

But Roar continued to worry.
He worried while he helped his mommy
roast vegetables in the garden.

He worried while he chased flocks of winged ponies off the roof.

And he worried while he washed his scales
and curled up to sleep.

The next morning, Roar waited at the bus stop with his mommy, daddy, and Sparkles

and worried

and worried

and worried

until

the bus

landed

at their

stop.

BUS

His mommy kissed him. His daddy kissed him.
And Sparkles took his hand and helped him climb onto the bus.

She held his hand through the loop-de-loops.
She held his hand through the landing.
And she held his hand all the way
to his classroom.

V IS FOR VOLCANO

Inside, Roar did not see any volcanos or knights in shining armor. Instead, he saw other little dragons playing with blocks and clay. And then he saw that his teacher was . . .

. . . a blue dragon with the biggest, toothiest, best smile he'd ever seen! "Hello, Roar!" she said. "I'm Mrs. Firestone."

"See? Everything will be okay," Sparkles said. She gave him a big hug and wrapped her tail around him before flying to her classroom.

Mrs. Firestone showed Roar to his very own chair next to a little purple dragon. "Roar, this is Scorch," the teacher said.
"Hello, Roar!" Scorch chirped.
"Hello," Roar said shyly.

In class, Roar and Scorch built a castle out of blocks.

In gym, they played
hide-and-seek-the-princess.

At lunch, they ate sandwiches charred to a yummy crisp.

And, at circle time, they listened to stories about Johnny Apple-dragon, who fried apple fritters at every state fair, and Cinder-dragonella, who skipped the ball and became a knight in shining scales who loved s'mores.

Near the end of the day, Mrs. Firestone gave everyone paper and crayons.
"Class, for our last activity today, I'd like you to draw a picture of something you love."

Roar thought about blocks and hide-and-seek and lunch with his new friend.
He thought about barbecues and sand castles and roasted vegetables.

And he drew
a very special
picture of
what he loved
most of all.

When he finished, the day
was over, and Sparkles
was at the classroom door
to walk with him back
to the bus.

"How was your first day,
Roar?" she asked.
"It was great!" he said.
"There was story time and
recess and blocks and I
made a new friend . . ."

Roar then told Sparkles about the very special drawing he'd made of what he loved most of all. "Can I see it?" she asked.

Roar carefully unfolded the paper.

"Roar, you drew me!" said Sparkles.

"Yes," he said, and Roar held Sparkles's
hand the whole bus ride home.

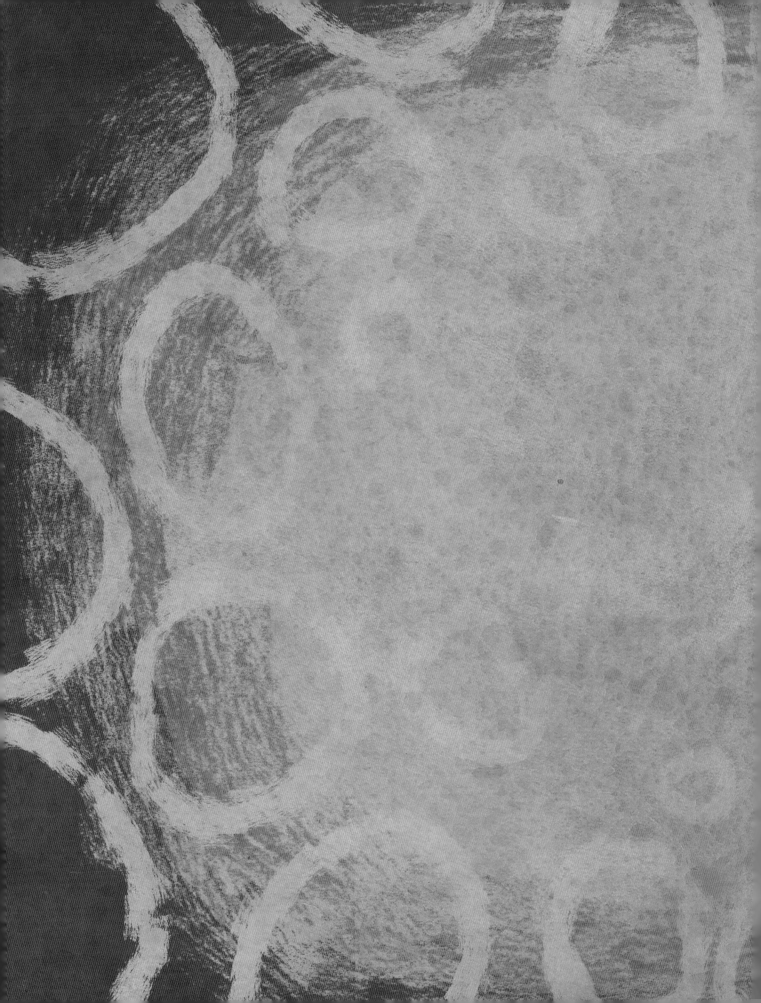